farfallina & marcel

HOLLY KELLER

GREENWILLOW BOOKS
An Imprint of HarperCollinsPublishers

AUTHOR'S NOTE

A butterfly is a beautiful insect that begins life as a caterpillar.
A mature butterfly lays eggs, and when the eggs hatch,
caterpillars are born. A caterpillar eats leaves and fruit and
grows very quickly. Because its skin does not grow with it,
a caterpillar will shed its skin several times, and each time will
grow a new and bigger one. After several weeks the caterpillar
begins the process of becoming a butterfly. It encases itself in
a protective covering called a cocoon, which hangs upside
down on a tree branch. Inside the cocoon the caterpillar changes
into a fully grown butterfly. Then the cocoon splits open and
the butterfly comes out.

Farfallina and Marcel
Copyright © 2002 by Holly Keller
All rights reserved. Manufactured in China by South China Printing Company Ltd.
www.harperchildrens.com

Watercolors were used for the full-color artwork.
The text type is Albertus MT.

Library of Congress Cataloging-in-Publication Data
Keller, Holly.
Farfallina and Marcel / Holly Keller.
    p.   cm.
"Greenwillow Books."
Summary: A caterpillar and a young goose become great friends, but as
they grow up they undergo changes which separate them for awhile.
ISBN 0-06-623932-X (trade). ISBN 0-06-623933-8 (lib. bdg)
ISBN 0-06-443872-4 (pbk.)
[I. Friendship—Fiction. 2. Growth—Fiction. 3. Caterpillars—Fiction.
4. Geese—Fiction.] I. Title.
PZ7.K28132 Far 2002   [E]—dc21   2001051297
10 9 8   First Edition

For Jon and Josie

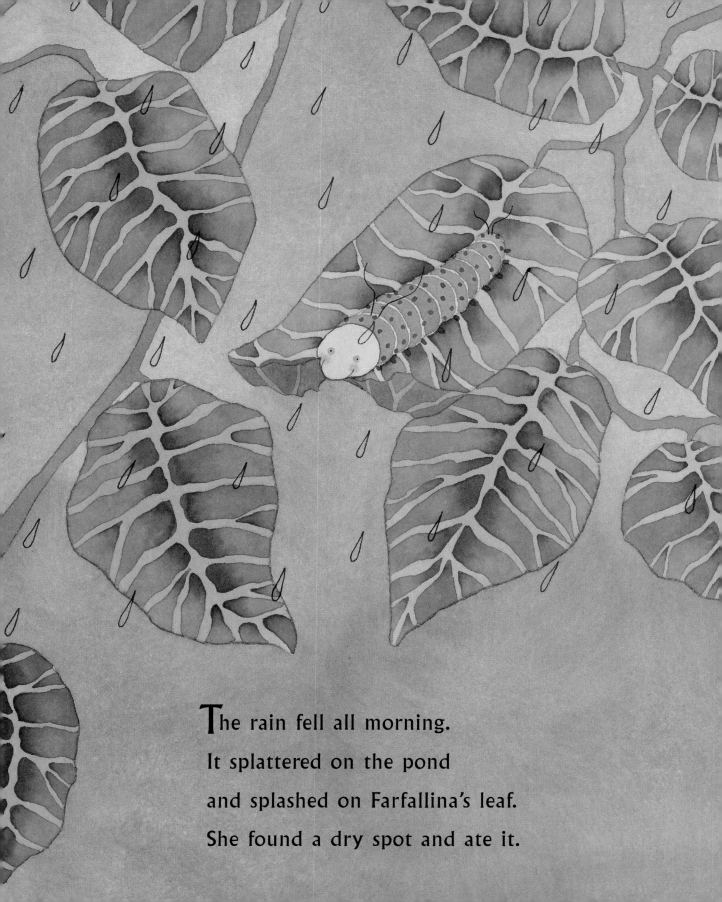

The rain fell all morning.
It splattered on the pond
and splashed on Farfallina's leaf.
She found a dry spot and ate it.

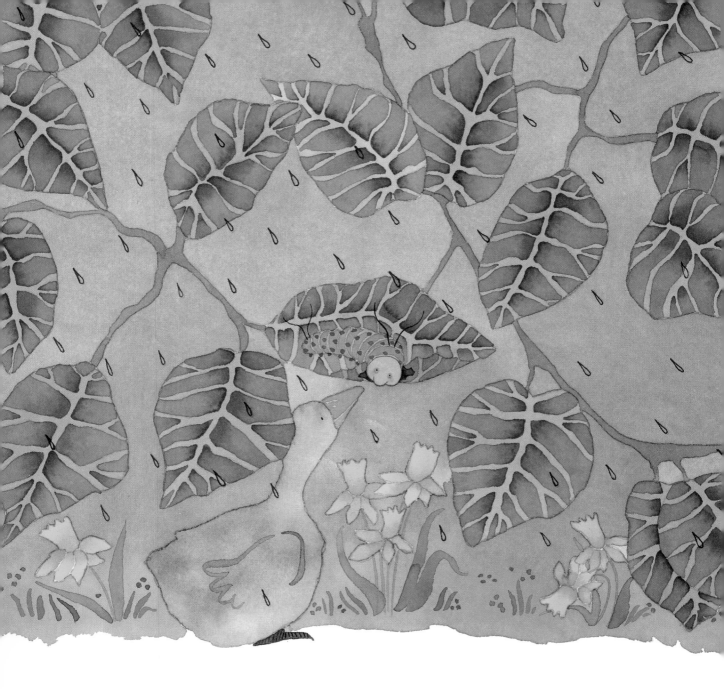

"Hey," said a little voice.

"You're eating my umbrella."

Farfallina peered over the edge.

A small gray bird was huddled underneath.

Farfallina liked his soft feathers and his gentle eyes.

"I'm Farfallina," she said,

and she slid down to the ground.

"My name is Marcel," said the bird.

He liked Farfallina's smile and her pretty colors.

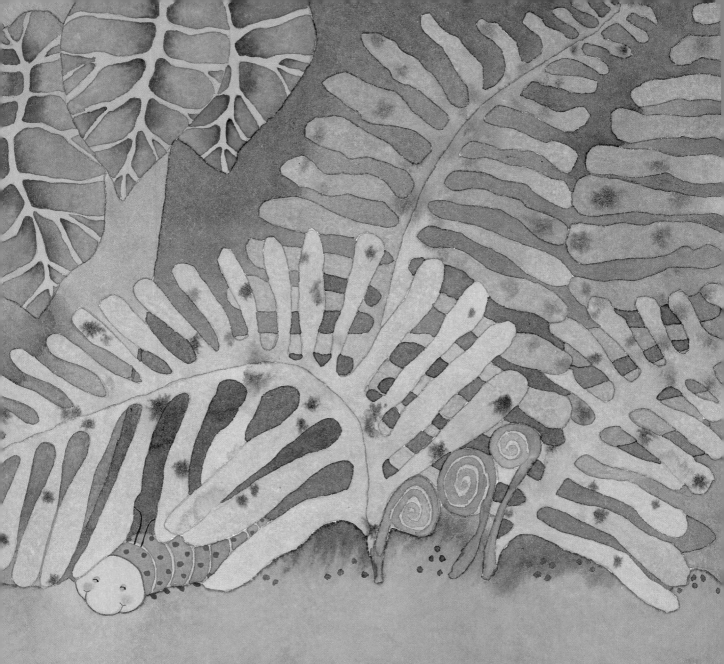

The rain turned to drizzle, and Farfallina wanted to play.

"I'll hide and you find me," she said.

Marcel agreed.

Farfallina hid under a fern close to the ground

because she knew that Marcel couldn't climb.

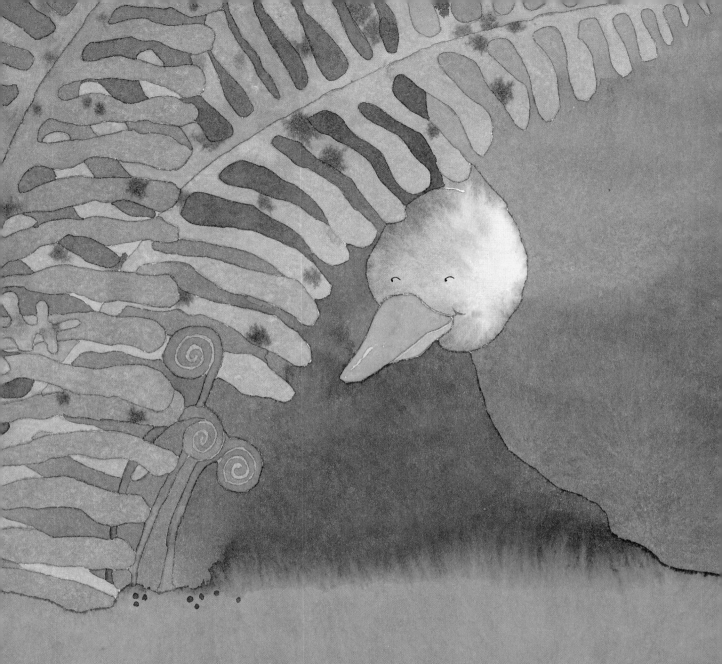

"Now I'll hide," said Marcel when he found her.
And he hid right behind the tree
because he knew that Farfallina moved slowly.

"I can take you for a ride on the pond," said Marcel.

Farfallina inched her way up to Marcel's back.

"You tickle," said Marcel, and he slipped into the water.

Farfallina giggled.
"There's so much to see,"
she said.

Farfallina and Marcel played together
every day. They liked the same games,
and they liked each other.
But one day Farfallina was not herself.
"I'm not sick," she told Marcel,
"just a little uncomfortable.
I need to climb up onto a branch
and rest for a while."
"I'll wait for you," Marcel called
as Farfallina made her way up the tree.
Marcel watched until Farfallina
was completely out of sight.
Then he settled himself in the grass
and waited.

Night came and then morning,
but Farfallina didn't come down.
Marcel called to her, but she didn't answer.
He was very worried and terribly lonely.

Weeks went by.

The afternoons grew longer and warmer,

and Marcel went to the pond.

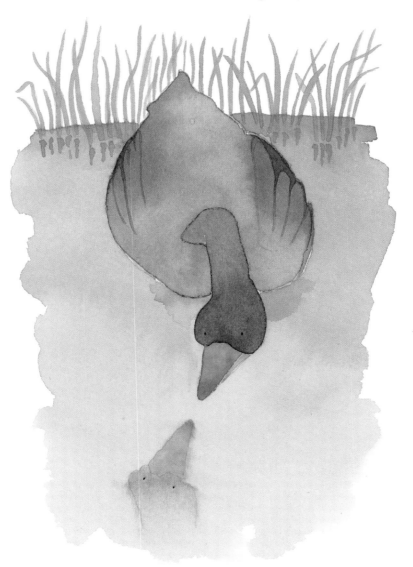

He was growing, and when he looked

at his reflection in the water,

he hardly recognized himself.

He went back to the tree every day
to look for Farfallina,
but she was never there.
And after a while he gave up.

At the top of the tree Farfallina was snuggled
in a blanket of glossy silk.
She was growing too.

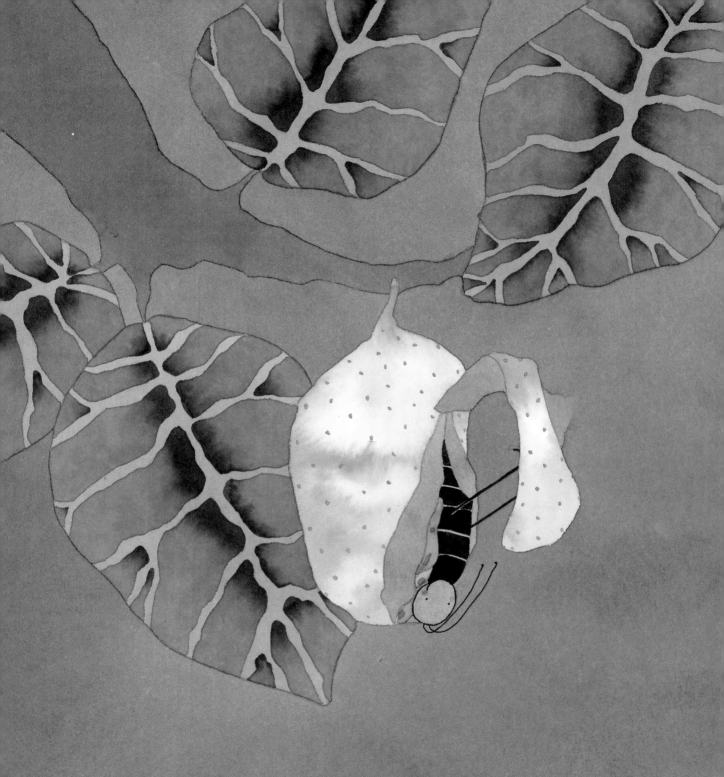

The sky was blue and clear the morning she was ready
to come out and open her beautiful new wings.

She had no idea how long she had been up in the tree,
and she floated down to find Marcel.

"I'll just wait," said Farfallina when she didn't see him,
and she sat on a flower.

Night came and then morning,
but Marcel wasn't there.
Farfallina was tired and confused.
She fluttered around a bit and went to the pond.

The pond was glassy smooth
except for the ripples
made by a large, handsome goose
who was swimming in solitary circles.
Farfallina shivered with disappointment.

She went to the pond every day
to look for the small gray bird named Marcel,
but he never came.
One morning the goose stopped his silent rounds
and spoke to her.
"You must like it here," he said.
Farfallina fluttered a bit.
"I've been waiting for a friend," she said sadly,
"but I don't think he'll come."

Marcel liked her smile and her brilliant colors.

"I know how you feel," he said. "I lost a friend too.

She just vanished into thin air."

Farfallina liked his sleek feathers and his gentle eyes.

"A ride around the pond might
cheer you up," Marcel said.
Farfallina thought it would, and she
settled herself on Marcel's back.

"It's funny," Marcel said, "but I feel as though
   I've known you a long time."
"I was just thinking the same thing," said Farfallina.
"My name is Farfallina. What's yours?"

Marcel stopped suddenly.

He beat the water with his strong wings.

Then he swam round and round and round.

"It's me, Farfallina," he shouted. "It's me, Marcel!

Is that really you?"

"It is," Farfallina shouted back.

They looked at each other and laughed.

By evening they had explained everything,
and they fell asleep smiling at the stars.

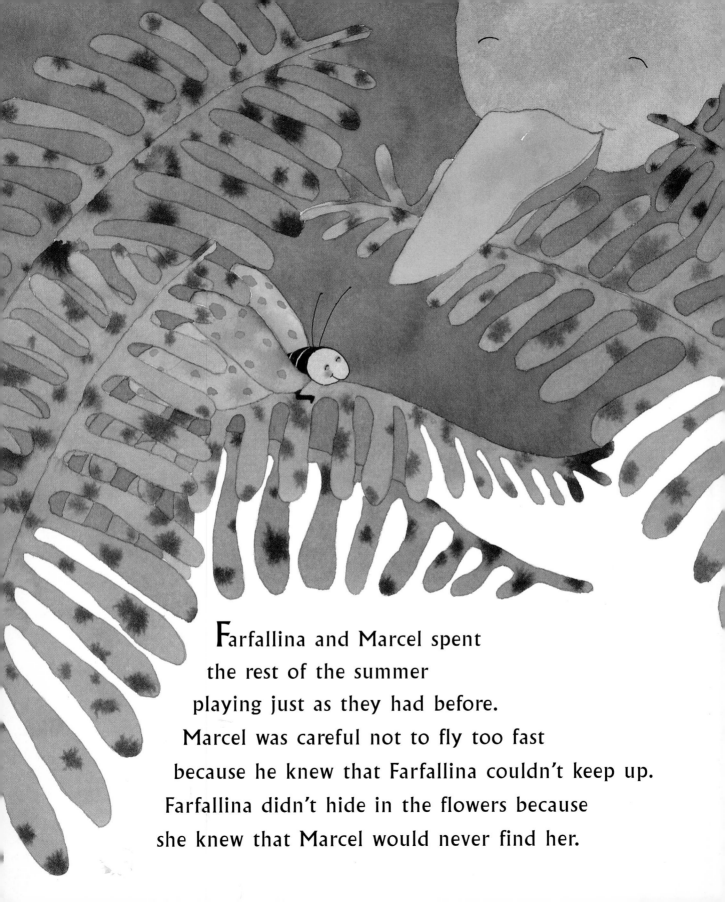

Farfallina and Marcel spent
the rest of the summer
playing just as they had before.
Marcel was careful not to fly too fast
because he knew that Farfallina couldn't keep up.
Farfallina didn't hide in the flowers because
she knew that Marcel would never find her.

And when the leaves on the trees
around the pond turned red and gold,
they decided to go south.

Together.